1st June 2007

The day the SAS found Madeleine's Kidnapper

1. 1st June 2007

Everyone will know the story of Madeleine McCann. The 3 year old child who disappeared from her bedroom in the Algarve. What few will know is that the joint SAS/MI5 Search Team located her kidnapper at the local mafia hotel. Tony Blair was in power then, and we need to know why he did not order her rescue. He is after all an elected official.

Undercover work is the forte of the Intelligence Agencies, and much of what they do does not reach the Press. Indeed the public are largely misinformed of what really goes on behind the scenes. Suffice to say that after the mysterious disappearance of this 3 year old British Subject probably the best covert operators in the business were tasked to solve it – the S.A.S. They really do deliver, whatever the cost.

Through a series of ingenious and fortuitous events, they were able to locate where the kidnapper came from. It should be no surprise that the Mafia were involved. They are probably the largest criminal organisation ignored, despite massive influence and power. Indeed they run certain Governments and are controlled elsewhere. Suffice to say all the dots fit together for anyone interested.

How the SAS located her goes beyond anything you might have imagined. It goes into the very depths of Intelligence Research where the moniker 'Above Top Secret' really exists. All that can be said at the present time is that the kidnapper was described in detail and location. Despite the best efforts of the Mafia he was then covertly identified at the local Mafia Hotel in Praia da Luz – the Vila Luz.

2. The Vila Luz

Scattered around the world are a series of semi obvious Mafia Hotels. Their reputation is known by the locals. Their design is similar. A place without Heart, built to a conformist design. They are a business and transact billions. Child kidnapping is the least of their activities. Quite how the organised abduction of the 3 year old child fits into this devious web is not in the least way obvious, unless you consider the very human nature of their bankers and how power corrupts.

Probably unknown to himself, Sergio Jardin was tagged by the SAS Team in June 2007, when they covertly searched his room, and found his explicit plans for Madeleine's abduction. The Mafia had moved him from the vicinity for almost a month to hide his tracks. Little did they know their mistake. Thus commenced a worldwide search into the activities of some of the largest criminal gangs on this planet. They thought they were safe with the best guarantee America can offer -the CIA. However even the CIA were fooled. In their arrogance they had thought that building one Head Mafia Hotel to coordinate their worldwide machinations was watertight. They were wrong.

In a very basic error, called hubris, they had miscalculated on a cosmic scale. Few people consider their inevitable mortality till it's too late. Even the most modest fool would see the signs of their being 'things unseen' in this life. However by definition criminals blind themselves with perishable trinkets. For this a price is paid.

3. PsiOps

In 1972, Ingo Swann successfully proved that there was a scientific foundation to PsiOps, at Stanford University under Dr Hal Puthoff. This CIA sponsored program was in response to the influencial book by Ostrander and Schroeder 'Psychic Discoveries behind the Iron Curtain'. This led to an exhaustive program that proved the points made by Carl Jung were with foundation. Basically it is possible to circumvent time.

Even today this work is little known, even hidden. It's consequences are enormous. The CIA renamed the program '8 Martini Technology'. It seems that we live in a coherent multidimensional Multiverse. No words can satisfactorially describe it, but experiences can. Today we live in a plethoria of New Knowledge that would seem to presage a New Age.

Using this Technology there are no secrets. In which case why is it not used to locate Madeleine McCann. Or perhaps it has been …

4. The Rothschilds

The Rothschilds basically run the world through a shadow government. They choose the leaders, policies and direction. Their worth has been calculated in the trillions by the Chinese Government. Thus Blair, Bush and Obama are their puppets. Their whole history has been theft, crime and lies. They stole their first £42m and were proven to be worth £1trillion eq in an 1850 Courtcase. Now it is possible to prove this, and they are not happy bunnies!

Princess Diana, 9/11, Kennedy. All now solved. David Icke had a mystical experience at Silustani where he was told that 'Great Secrets will be unveiled'. Now you will find out why life is made so deliberately difficult to line the pockets of a corrupt elite. You will even find that Cancer Cures have been deliberately concealed via death threats. Worth the cost of this book alone!

The instigator of the Madeleine McCann abduction is a 'mega rich whitehaired old man who walks the corridors of power in Whitehall'. Sound familiar? Even the SAS/MI5 Team were shocked not just by this information, but where it came from …

5. Where is she now?

Even a quick read so far will have given you much food for thought. But the question is where is she now? Consider that the chief advisors in the whole case have been Whitehall employees, and a plot develops.

Clearly the ability to locate her is there. There are many permutations but one thing is clear. When Kate and Gerry sought out help from the Catholic Church it was a desperate measure. Perhaps they should have looked more carefully at their bankers and what underlies the Mason's. There are clearly hidden Forces that pervade our lifes that few consider. However if the Golden Dawn was correct then it's Prophet would have been W.B.Yeats.

6. The Rocking Cradle

<u>William Butler Yeats (1865-1939)</u>

THE SECOND COMING

Turning and turning in the widening gyre
The falcon cannot hear the falconer;
Things fall apart; the centre cannot hold;
Mere anarchy is loosed upon the world,
The blood-dimmed tide is loosed, and everywhere
The ceremony of innocence is drowned;
The best lack all conviction, while the worst
Are full of passionate intensity.

Surely some revelation is at hand;
Surely the Second Coming is at hand.
The Second Coming! Hardly are those words out
When a vast image out of Spiritus Mundi
Troubles my sight: a waste of desert sand;
A shape with lion body and the head of a man,
A gaze blank and pitiless as the sun,
Is moving its slow thighs, while all about it
Wind shadows of the indignant desert birds.

The darkness drops again but now I know
That twenty centuries of stony sleep
Were vexed to nightmare by a rocking cradle,
And what rough beast, its hour come round at last,
Slouches towards Bethlehem to be born?

The Day After Roswell

A Former Pentagon Official Reveals the U.S. Government's Shocking UFO Cover-Up

by Colonel Philip Corso

"To say this is a significant book, if not *the* most significant book to appear on a UFO subject in decades can hardly be considered an exageration. If even a portion of Corso's extraordinary claims are true, the implications are staggering. Corso has told a fascinating story, at times cinematic, with enough meat to keep UFO researchers chewing for years to come."

-- Peter Jordon, *UFO Magazine*

Colonel Corso's background:

Military officer during World War II and Army intelligence officer on General Douglas MacArthur's staff during the Korean War; member of the President Eisenhower's National Security Council as a Lt. Colonel for four years; head of Foreign Technology in Army Research and Development at the Pentagon in the early 1960s, where he was in charge of the Roswell Files, the cache of UFO parts and information which "an Army retrieval team . . . pulled out of the wreckage of a flying disk that had crashed outside the town of Roswell in the New Mexico desert in the early-morning darkness during the first week of July 1947."; retired from the Army in 1963 with nineteen medals and ribbons; then served as National Security specialist staff to U.S. Senators James Eastland and Strom Thurmond; and subsequently has worked as a consultant and contracts administrator in the private sector.

Revelations:

Colonel Corso tells that there were five extraterrestrials, 4-1/2 feet tall with greyish-brown skin, four-fingered hands and oversized hairless heads, found at the Roswell UFO crash site, two of them still alive. One tried to run away and was shot by nervous soldiers. The other was still alive but dying when he arrived in the back of an Army truck at Roswell Army Air Field. He was Post Duty Officer at Fort Riley, Kansas in 1947, the night a shipment of Roswell artifacts arrived from Fort Bliss. Colonel Corso examined the shipment, which included one of the dead extraterrestrials preserved in a thick light-blue liquid. The shipment was destined for what is now called Wright-Patterson Air Force Base, Ohio. Corso speaks about serving in President Eisenhower's National Security Council, and seeing the memos about the Roswell incident and the "goods" retrieved from it.

The Colonel divulges how he spearheaded the Army's supersecret reverse-engineering project that "seeded" extraterrestrial technology at American corporations such as IBM, Hughes Aircraft, Bell Labs, and Dow Corning - without their knowledge. He describes the devices found aboard the

Roswell craft, and how they became the precursors for today's integrated circuit chips, fibre optics, lasers, night-vision equipment, super-tenacity fibers (such as Kevlar plastic armor), and classified discoveries, such as psychotronic devices that can translate human thoughts into signals that control machinery, Stealth aircraft technology, and Star Wars particle-beam devices. He also discusses the role that extraterrestrial technology played in shaping geopolitical policy and events; how it helped the United States surpass the Russians in space; spurred elaborate Army initiatives such as SDI (Star Wars Projects), Project Horizon (to place a military base on the Moon), and HAARP; and ultimately brought about the end of the Cold War.

Colonel Corso also said that captured UFOs were/are kept at Norton, Edwards and Nellis (Area 51) Air Force Bases. He said a UFO Working Group was set up by President Truman in September, 1947, a group some call MJ-12, and that it has functioned ever since. In the 1950s two crude prototypes of antigravity craft were constructed, but were powered by crude human nuclear fission generators, and were inefficient and leaked radiation. He says that the Star Wars program was always primarily to prepare for war against the extraterrestrials in case of invasion.

8. Mystery Religions

Throughout history knowledge has been power, and non is greater than the mysteries of existence. It is as if we have lost the 'Manual for Life'. Certain groups have suffered tremendous persecution for rediscovering some of the keys. One of these have been the Sufi's.

They are a mysterious group but the Spiritual Guide 'Daughter of Fire' by Irina Tweedie describes a Path that works. It describes how humans can rise to another higher level, that is currently rare. 2012 is one of the Key Dates in their predictions. We are in the midst of their dynamic predictions where we have Collective choices. Do we sit back and see what happens, or do we follow our hearts?

9. A New Science

One of the Great Hidden Discoveries is a Machine that can see the Human Aura. This has been spoken about for generations but ignored by science. Now there is a machine that can see it!

Mr Oldfield developed it by himself using the developments of Tesla. It replicates all the descriptions of the ancient Indian Texts, yet is ignored by Science.

It pretty well proves we live in a multidimensional energy based Mulitverse. When you see what it can do you will understand why it has been ignored.

http://www.electrocrystal.com/

10. Choices

What sort of World do you want?

Who do you think will make it happen?

When will it happen?

Answer this and solve the Madeleine McCann Mystery

The End.